Len Lucero and
Kristina Tracy

Chris P. Bacon

My Life So Far...

Illustrated by
Penny Weber

HAY HOUSE, INC.
Carlsbad, California • New York City
London • Sydney • Johannesburg
Vancouver • Hong Kong • New Delhi

Copyright © 2013 by Len Lucero

Published and distributed in the United States by: Hay House, Inc.: www.hayhouse.com® • **Published and distribued in Australia by:** Hay House Australia Pty. Ltd.: www.hayhouse.com .au • **Published and distributed in the United Kingdom by:** Hay House UK, Ltd.: www.hayhouse.co.uk • **Published and distributed in the Republic of South Africa by:** Hay House SA (Pty), Ltd.: www.hayhouse.co.za • **Distributed in Canada by:** Raincoast: www.raincoast.com • **Published in India by:** Hay House Publishers India: www.hayhouse.co.in

Editorial assistance and interior design: Jenny Richards • *Illustrations:* © Penny Weber • *Interior photos:* © Len Lucero

Library of Congress Control Number: 2013944863

Hardcover ISBN: 978-1-4019-4439-1

16 15 14 13   5 4 3 2

1st edition, November 2013
2nd edition, November 2013

Printed in China

This book is dedicated to all of the fans and followers of Chris P. Bacon. Chris P.'s fans have become such a big part of our lives, and their love, enthusiasm, and kind words made this book possible. Thank you!

— Len Lucero

I'm not very old, just a little piglet,
but my life sure has been exciting so far!
You see, my name is Chris P. Bacon. I know . . .
funny name for a pig. Maybe you've heard
of me or seen me on TV? Well, if not, let
me start from the beginning . . .

My first memory is of the day I was taken to the veterinarian's office. You probably know this, but a veterinarian is a doctor who takes care of animals. Anyway, I remember being handed to a kind-looking man named Dr. Len who smelled like cinnamon. He looked into my eyes and smiled and said, "You can come home with me, and we'll have a good life together."

As we drove home that night, Dr. Len—or Dad, as I call him now—explained something to me that I had been wondering about. "You are a special pig. Your back legs don't work like most pigs, but that's okay. You are UNIQUE." *Hmmm...* I thought. I like the sound of that... Yooooo-neek! "Oink-Oink," I said.

yooooo-neek!

HOME!

When we got home and
I saw all the animals
that were going to be my
new pals—like Duma (the cat) and
Aspen (the dog)—I squeeeeealed with
delight. Dr. Len's family welcomed me
with hugs and kisses, and I knew I was
going to like it there!

It had been the longest day of my short life, and I was tired, so I curled up by the warm fire in a pile of snuggly blankets and drifted off to a happy sleep. I dreamed of playing with my new family and being set free in a pie shop!

In the morning, after a breakfast of oatmeal topped with blueberries (yum!), Dad showed me a funny-looking thing with wheels. It looked like a toy!

"This is for you, Chris—it's a cart. I made it to hold up your back legs so you can run around and play." *How awesome*, I thought. "Oink-Oink," I said.

Dad put the cart on me, and I could stand up, but boy was it hard to get going at first. The straps felt strange, and my wheels kept popping up in the air. But after lots of practice, and with everyone cheering me on, I was rolling!

A few weeks later, while I was trying to get a
marshmallow out from under the couch, Dad shouted,
"Look, Chris! You're on YouTube." I popped my head up,
and sure enough, there I was! I guess Dad had posted
a video of my first try with my cart. After that, the
phone would not stop ringing. It seemed like everyone
had seen my video and thought I was the cutest,
most bravest pig ever!

Boy, did my life get busy after that! Everyone wanted to know about me and my cart. I got to visit lots of TV shows in different cities and make all kinds of new friends. People kept calling me "Inspiring," which I think means that I make them feel like they want to do their very best.

KEEP ON ROLLING! ♥ COLE

NEVER GIVE UP!

TV

All I want to do is make people smile, and Dad says I do that all the time. It seems to me that if you make people smile, it puts them in a good mood... and if you're in a good mood, it's easier to think positive... and if you think positive, who knows what you can do?! Or in other words, Oinkity-Oink-Oink-Oink!

Chris P.
you inspire me!!
xoxo

Cute!
Positive!!
Brave!

Traveling all over has been a great adventure.
I even went to New York City, stayed in a hotel
room, and had a hot fudge sundae delivered to
my door!

Being famous is all really fun and exciting,
but now I'm happy to be back home with
my family, playing with Aspen and Duma
and getting as dirty as possible.

The best thing about my new life is that
I get to meet people and animals who
are different...just like me. I think that
when they see what a tiny pink pig can do
with a little help—and a lot of grunting—
it makes them realize that they can do all
kinds of things, too. It's cool to be

yooooo-neek!

BABY DAYS

FRIENDS!

HAPPY TIMES!

We hope you enjoyed this Hay House book. If you'd like to receive our online catalog featuring additional information on Hay House books and products, or if you'd like to find out more about the Hay Foundation, please contact:

Hay House, Inc.
P.O. Box 5100
Carlsbad, CA 92018-5100

(760) 431-7695 or **(800) 654-5126**
(760) 431-6948 (fax) or **(800) 650-5115 (fax)**
www.hayhouse.com® • www.hayfoundation.org

Published and distributed in Australia by: Hay House Australia Pty. Ltd., 18/36 Ralph St., Alexandria NSW 2015
Phone: 612-9669-4299 • Fax: 612-9669-4144 • www.hayhouse.com.au

Published and distributed in the United Kingdom by: Hay House UK, Ltd., Astley House, 33 Notting Hill Gate, London W11 3JQ
Phone: 44-20-3675-2450 • Fax: 44-20-3675-2451 • www.hayhouse.co.uk

Published and distributed in the Republic of South Africa by: Hay House SA (Pty), Ltd.,
P.O. Box 990, Witkoppen 2068 • Phone/Fax: 27-11-467-8904 • www.hayhouse.co.za

Published in India by: Hay House Publishers India, Muskaan Complex, Plot No. 3, B-2, Vasant Kunj,
New Delhi 110 070 • Phone: 91-11-4176-1620 • Fax: 91-11-4176-1630 • www.hayhouse.co.in

Distributed in Canada by: Raincoast, 9050 Shaughnessy St., Vancouver, B.C. V6P 6E5
Phone: (604) 323-7100 • Fax: (604) 323-2600 • www.raincoast.com